MISS BUTTERPAT GOES WILD!

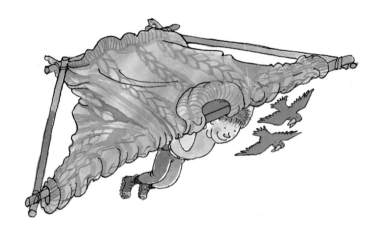

Malcolm Yorke

with illustrations by
Margaret Chamberlain

DORLING KINDERSLEY

LONDON • NEW YORK • STUTTGART

A DORLING KINDERSLEY BOOK

First American Edition, 1993
2 4 6 8 10 9 7 5 3 1

Published in the United States by
Dorling Kindersley, Inc., 232 Madison Avenue
New York, New York 10016

Library of Congress Cataloging-in-Publication Data
Yorke, Malcolm, 1938-
Miss Butterpat goes wild / by Malcolm Yorke ; illustrated by
Margaret Chamberlain. —1st American ed.
p. cm. — (Teachers' secrets)
Summary: Miss Butterpat's students don't believe that she spent her summer in a
series of adventures, including a trip to South America, living with Indians in the
jungle, and winning a fortune in a poker game.
ISBN 1-56458-200-0
[1. Teachers—Fiction. 2. Adventure and adventurers—Fiction.
3. Humorous stories.] I. Chamberlain, Margaret. i11. II. Title.
III. Series.
PZ7.Y8244M1 1993
[Fic]—dc20
93-20204
CIP
AC

Color reproduction by DOT Gradations Ltd.
Printed in Singapore

Miss Cushy Butterpat was a teacher. She sat in the school staff room each lunchtime, sipping tea, nibbling caramel candies, and knitting a large, blue sweater. All the staff and students thought she was a wonderful person, but perhaps a little bit dull.

It was the last day of the school year and summer vacation was about to begin. Miss Butterpat said to her class:

"Now children, I hope you all have a lovely summer and do lots of super things. When we meet again in September, I'll want to hear all about your adventures."

AND MY AUNTIE'S COMING FROM TRINIDAD.

I'M GOING CAMPING IN VIRGINIA.

"Your plans sound wonderful," she said.

"What are you going to do, Miss Butterpat?" asked Susan.

"Me? Oh well, I thought I might stow away on a ship to South America, explore the jungle, live with a tribe of Indians, canoe down a river – that sort of thing. . . . "

The class laughed and laughed.

"You do tell whoppers, Miss Butterpat," said Leroy. And they all went off to their holidays, giggling at their teacher's little joke.

The next morning, Cushy Butterpat cut her hair very short and put on her jeans, some sturdy boots, and her big, blue sweater. She packed her backpack and took a train to New Orleans.

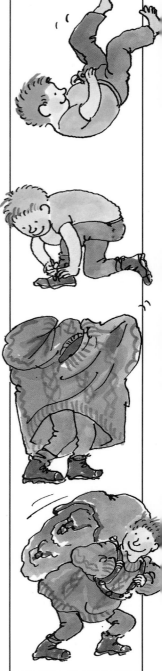

On the train, she went into the bathroom. When she came out, she was wearing a false beard and moustache.

She arrived in New Orleans where she met the captain of a cargo boat, the S.S. *Saucy Rachel.* She told the captain that her name was Charlie and that she would make a good deckhand on his voyage to South America.

"OK, join the crew," said the captain.

The other sailors thought Charlie was
tough and hardworking. He could
also play the tin whistle, drink rum,
and play cards with the best of them.

The little cargo boat was tossed around by a wild typhoon, but at last it arrived safely in South America. Charlie helped unload the cargo, said good-bye to the crew, and set off for the nearest town.

There was a carnival in town. Everybody was wearing fantastic costumes and parading through the streets. Cushy wanted to join in, so she threw away her beard and became Cushy Butterpat again.

She stretched her big, blue sweater and made herself look like an elephant by putting an arm down one sleeve for a trunk, and using the other for a tail.

"I know, I'll use some leaves for ears," thought Cushy. "And some rolled up paper for tusks."

She had a wonderful time in the parade. Afterward, she danced the rhumba, the cha-cha, and the lambada until dawn.

11

That morning, Cushy caught a rusty old steamboat up the local river. As the boat went farther and farther into the jungle, she could see monkeys and parrots in the trees and hear the calls of the jaguars and even the hiss of the snakes.

"This looks good," thought Cushy as she got off the boat. "I'm off to explore the jungle!"

OLD RUSTY

Cushy was feeling very hot in her big, blue sweater as she pushed her way through the leafy jungle. Suddenly, she was gripped by a huge boa constrictor. It began to coil around her, ready to squeeze her to death!

Fortunately, the blue sweater was so big and loose that Cushy was able to slip out of it before the squeeze got too tight. The puzzled snake found it had only an empty blue skin in its grip, so it slid off to find a less slippery victim.

Cushy Butterpat plodded on, nibbling berries and her supply of caramel candies during the day, and camping out at night.

She came to another river. It was too wide and fast for her to swim across.

"How am I going to cross this?" Cushy wondered. "I know . . ."

She took off her sweater and pushed a branch through both arm holes. She pushed other branches across the sides and waist until it looked like the sail of a hang glider. Then she jumped from a tree and . . . "Wheeeeee!"

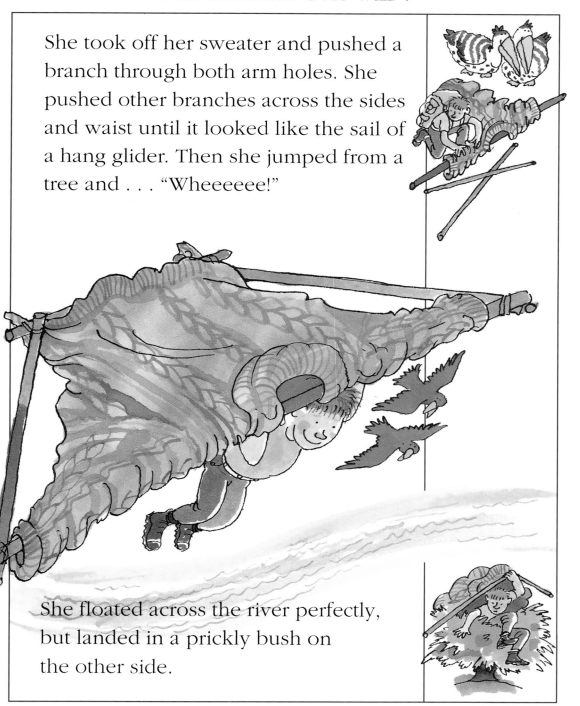

She floated across the river perfectly, but landed in a prickly bush on the other side.

Cushy went on until she came to a village. The local Indians had never ever met anyone like her before, but they were very friendly.

"You are a nice lady. You join our tribe?" they suggested.

"Thank you very much," said Cushy.

It was so hot in the village that Cushy didn't need her sweater any more. She unravelled part of it to make fishing lines. Another square of it was made into a butterfly net. Other bits went into necklaces or hair ribbons, and she taught the children how to play cat's cradle and fly a kite.

She joined her new friends when they fished and went hunting with spears and bows and arrows.

She helped cook the food, amused the children, and was particularly good at playing the drums.

Eventually, Cushy remembered that she ought to be getting back home. The tribe was sad to see her go, but they gave her a canoe as a good-bye present.

"Bye-bye, everyone," she called, and they cheered as she set off down the river.

For several days she paddled along the river. A crocodile thought she looked like a tasty treat. "Shoo!" she said as she smacked it on the head with her paddle.

At the first big town, Cushy landed and sold her canoe. With the money, she joined in a poker game. She played against a wicked bandit called Jake and managed to win his horse, saddle, a gun, and a big bag of gold.

"I'm gonna get you, lady," said the evil
Jake, as he pointed his other pistol at
her. But Cushy was quick. She shot a
hole in his hat before he could even
take aim.

Then she leaped onto the horse
and galloped off out of town.

Eventually, Cushy reached the port again. She used her bag of gold to buy a first-class ticket on a ship bound for home.

What luxury! She sunbathed and swam in the pool. She ate delicious food, and every evening she danced the tango, the waltz, and the fox-trot!

"Marry me!" said all the men passengers
who had fallen madly in love with her.
They threatened to jump overboard
if she did not dance with them.
She told them all not to be so silly.

At last, Cushy reached New Orleans once again. She went to visit her granny and spent the last few days of her vacation mowing her granny's lawn and weeding her garden.

Every afternoon they had tea and caramel candies while Granny told Cushy all the local gossip. Her old gran did not once ask Cushy how she had spent the rest of her holiday.

When Cushy Butterpat went back
to school in September, the other
teachers were very chatty.

MY, YOU
LOOK TAN,
CUSHY !

I'M NOT SURE
THAT NEW
HAIRSTYLE
SUITS YOU.

YOU'VE LOST
A BIT OF
WEIGHT.

Then they all told her about their
vacations in New York, Spain, and
Los Angeles. Nobody bothered to ask
Miss Butterpat what **she** had been
doing all summer.

Cushy's class told her all about **their** summers.

I SAW COWS BEING MILKED.

I LEARNED HOW TO COUNT TO TEN IN FRENCH.

OUR COUSINS HAVE FUNNY AUSTRALIAN ACCENTS.

MY AUNTIE COOKED US REAL WEST INDIAN FOOD!

Cushy listened to them all with great interest. Then Susan said, "And what did **you** do, Miss Butterpat?"

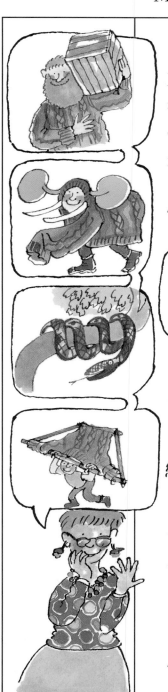

"Me? Oh well, I wore a beard and pretended to be a sailor, took part in a carnival as a blue elephant, escaped from a boa constrictor, made a hang glider, and . . . "

They all laughed and laughed.

YOU'RE FOOLING US AGAIN !

IT'S NOT STORYTIME YET !

GO ON, MISS BUTTERPAT TELL US WHAT YOU REALLY DID.

"Well, I also stayed with my granny and mowed her lawn and weeded her garden," said Miss Butterpat with a sigh.

"That's more like it," the children said.

This time they believed her.

That same lunchtime Miss Butterpat sat in the staffroom, sipping her tea and nibbling her caramel candies. She also began to knit another huge sweater. This time a red one.

It would keep her warm next year, when she climbed Mount Everest.